Joseph,

Read often, Play a
lot, and laugh at least
once every day!

Francine Poppo Rich
2/17/05

Why Can't I Spray Today?

By Francine Poppo Rich
Illustrated by Thomas H. Bone' III

A PeeWee Pipes Adventure

Blue Marlin Publications

Why Can't I Spray Today?

Published by Blue Marlin Publications

Text copyright © 1999 by Francine Poppo Rich

Illustrations copyright © 1999 by Francine Poppo Rich

First printing, December 1999

ISBN 0-9674602-0-4

Blue Marlin Publications, Ltd.
823 Aberdeen Road, West Bay Shore, NY 11706
Http://www.bluemarlinpubs.com

Printed and Bound by Friesens Book Division in Altona, Manitoba, Canada

Special thanks to Cheryl Royer, Ginny & Pher Reinman, and Jerry W. Dragoo, Ph.D. for their assistance and expert information on skunks and skunk behavior.

For Daddy

Father Funk is Mr. Skunk and
Mamma Mist is Mrs. Skunk.

PeeWee Pipes is their son
whose tail sprayer is still very young.

PeeWee Pipes loves being a skunk
so much that he wiggles and prances

and toe-taps
and dances.

He rumbles and tumbles

and gets all in a jumble.

He slips and slides.

And when he hides, nobody (not even Father Funk or Mamma Mist) can find him.

But PeeWee Pipes is very sad today
because he cannot get his tail
sprayer to spray.

When he tries to spray and act tough,
all that comes out is a
sizzly puff.

So he swings his tail and whips it about
and tries to make it spray and spout.

He squeezes and squeezes and squeezes.

But nothing, nothing will come out.

So PeeWee Pipes runs all the way
home to tell Father and Mamma
that something is very wrong.

"Father, Mamma," he huffs, "my tail sprayer won't spray. I haven't been able to spray today."

Father Funk and Mamma Mist tell PeeWee to remember this: "Your spray is your weapon to keep safe in your pouch. You may use it only when you're afraid or in danger.

Otherwise, you must never try to make it come out."

"When you need to keep a coyote or spotted owl away, we promise your sprayer will spray. Now please do as we say and keep your sprayer tucked away."

So PeeWee Pipes keeps his spray in his pouch. He
never tries to make it come out
because he knows he may need it someday
to keep danger away.

PeeWee Pipes still loves being a skunk
so much that he be-bops and bounces

and parades and pounces on beetles and
barley and grass and grubs.

He slips

and slides.

And when he hides,

nobody (not even Father Funk or Mamma Mist) can find him!

Photo of Jezebel, courtesy of Pher Reinman

Born deaf and blind and weighing approximately one ounce, newborn skunks are only about four inches long. That's the weight and length of a small, toy car! They are also born with no fur, and their skin is pink and white. After a day or two, black fur grows on the pink skin, and white fur grows on the white skin. A fully-grown skunk is about as long and heavy as a newborn, human baby.

Six species of skunks live in the United States: the Gulf Coast and Common Hognosed Skunks, the Hooded Skunk, the Eastern and Western Spotted Skunks, and the Striped Skunk. They live in places such as hollow trees, city backyards, and near ponds. They can swim the dog paddle, run, and play. Their favorite food is insects (especially beetles, crickets, and grasshoppers). They are helpful to humans because they eat many insects that are harmful to us. Skunks will spray their foul-smelling liquid, but only if provoked. And they will warn the intruder first by stamping their feet and hissing or growling.

Skunks can make great pets; they are extremely intelligent, stubborn, loving animals who enjoy playing with balls, newspapers, stuffed toys, and even garbage (yuk)!